Vehicles
On The Move

Vehicles on the
FARM

Lynn Peppas

🌳 Crabtree Publishing Company

www.crabtreebooks.com

Created by Bobbie Kalman

Dedicated By Crystal Sikkens
To my husband John, my favourite farmer

Author
Lynn Peppas

Editorial director
Kathy Middleton

Project editor
Paul Challen

Editor
Adrianna Morganelli

Proofreaders
Rachel Stuckey
Crystal Sikkens

Photo research
Melissa McClellan

Design
Tibor Choleva
Melissa McCLellan

Production coordinators
Katherine Berti
Margaret Amy Salter

Prepress technician
Katherine Berti

Consultant
Mary Dawson, Farm Equipment Sales Representative

Special thanks to
Jonathan Sikkens

Illustrations
All illustrations by Leif Peng

Photographs
BigStockPhoto.com: © Chris Roselli (back cover, page 31)
Dreamstime.com: © Randy Mckown (page 5 middle); © Jennifer Thompson (page 8); © Sonya Etchison (page 10); © Marcin Husiatynski (page 11)
istockphoto.com: © Dan Driedger (16–17); © Cameron Pashak (page 30)
Photos.com: front cover
Shutterstock.com: © Orientaly (title page) ; © Luis Louro (table of contents page); © Tish1 (pages 4–5, 22); © Andresr (page 5 top); © Krivosheev Vitaly (page 6); © Marilyn Barbone (page 7 bottom); © Inginsh (page9); © Cappi Thompson (pages 12–13); © haak78 (page 14); © Horst Kanzek (page 15); © Desha Cam (page 17 top); © Niels Quist (page 18); © s74 (page 19 top); © Michael Hieber (page 19 bottom); © Maksud (pages 20–21); © Daniel Alvarez (page 23 top); © Sally Scott (page 23 bottom); © Tyler Olson (page 24 top); © ilFede (pages 24–25); © Ermes (page 25 top); © Denton Rumsey (page 26); © Phillip Minnis (page 27); © Daniel Yordanov (pages 28–29)
© Stu Harrding (page 12 top)
© Melissa McClellan (page 7 top)

Library and Archives Canada Cataloguing in Publication

Peppas, Lynn
	Vehicles on the farm / Lynn Peppas.

(Vehicles on the move)
Includes index.
Issued also in an electronic format.
ISBN 978-0-7787-3051-4 (bound).--ISBN 978-0-7787-3065-1 (pbk.)

	1. Agricultural machinery--Juvenile literature. I. Title. II. Series:
Vehicles on the move

S675.25.P46 2011   j631.3   C2010-904806-7

Library of Congress Cataloging-in-Publication Data

CIP available at Library of Congress

Crabtree Publishing Company

www.crabtreebooks.com   1-800-387-7650

Printed in the U.S.A./082010/BA20100709

Published in Canada
Crabtree Publishing
616 Welland Ave.
St. Catharines, ON
L2M 5V6

Published in the United States
Crabtree Publishing
PMB 59051
350 Fifth Avenue, 59th Floor
New York, New York 10118

Published in the United Kingdom
Crabtree Publishing
Maritime House
Basin Road North, Hove
BN41 1WR

Published in Australia
Crabtree Publishing
386 Mt. Alexander Rd.
Ascot Vale (Melbourne)
VIC 3032

Contents

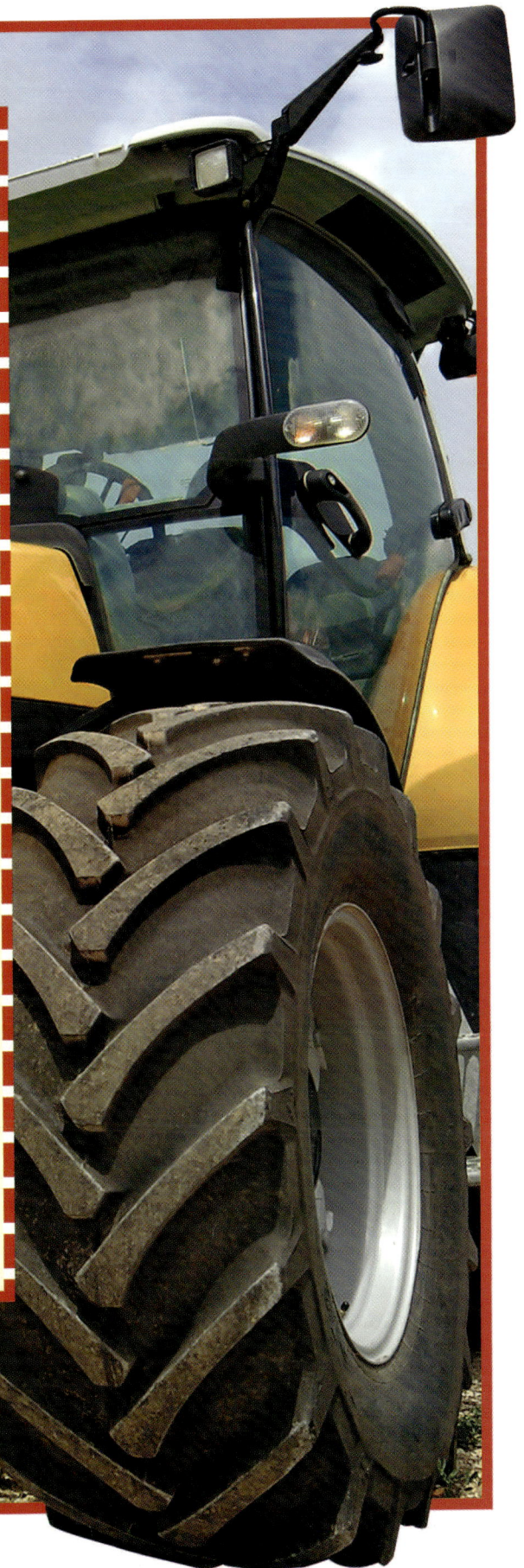

Working on the farm

It takes a lot of hard work to run a farm. Farmers have many different vehicles to help them do the job. Vehicles are machines that move and do work. Farm machines have to be powerful and tough.

harvested corn

trailer

tractor

Modern-day helpers

We get our food from farms. Grocery stores would be empty if there were no farms.

Long ago, animals helped people do work on a farm. Today, farm vehicles can do much more work than animals and in less time.

A family buying fresh fruit

Horses pulling a small plow

combine harvester

corn field

Tough tractors

Tractors are rugged vehicles. They have to be to work on all kinds of surfaces. They work in all kinds of weather. They pull, lift, and push heavy machines. They help do many different jobs on a farm.

cab

engine

front-end weights

wheels

Hitching it up

Tractors have a **hitch** in the back so that other pieces of farm equipment can be attached to them. Farm machines that need power to run attach to the power take-off, or **PTO**, in the back of a tractor. They are powered by the tractor's engine.

three-point hitch

power take-off

a closer look

hay rake connected to the PTO

The PTO on a tractor or truck is used to provide power to a separate farm machine. It can be easily connected and disconnected.

7

Many jobs

Tractors do more jobs on a farm than any other vehicle. They take care of crops throughout the growing season. Tractors prepare the soil for planting. They plant the seeds. They help control insects. They help harvest, or bring in, the crops. They help turn crops into feed for animals and people. They do it all!

Tractors on farms often work in teams to get the job done quickly.

Always on the go

Tractors never stop. They work all year long. They clear land of trees, stack bales of hay, and even plow snow during the winter months. They are hard-working vehicles.

All tractors have strong headlights that allow them to work at night.

Big wheels

Tractors have big rubber wheels with deep treads. Treads are patterns in the wheel that help it grip muddy or sandy surfaces. Heavy vehicles can crush the soil and crops. A tractor's big wheels help to carry its weight over a large area so it does not harm the soil. Tractors can have four, six, eight, or even twelve wheels.

big rubber wheel

Tractor tires are huge. Some tires are taller than a person standing.

On track

Some tractors have tracks instead of wheels. They are called **crawler tractors**. Tracks help carry even more weight and do less damage to soil and crops.

wide track

Crawler tractor tracks are made of rubber. They have deep treads. Crawler tractors easily drive over any kind of surface.

Extra-large farms need monster-sized tractors. One of the biggest farm tractors in the world is the Big Bud 747. It is over 14 feet (4.2 m) tall. The wheels alone are eight feet (2.4 m) tall.

One size does not fit all

Tractors come in different sizes for different sizes of jobs. **CUT** stands for compact utility tractor. These small tractors are the perfect size for golf courses and the gardens and yards of large estate homes. Most farms have standard-sized tractors. They have a lot of power. They can turn and move easily.

Compact utility tractors are used to cut the greens at a golf course.

Groundbreaking plow

A **plow** breaks up soil. Soil forms a hard crust on top. A plow digs into the ground with sharp, metal blades that cut into the soil and turn it over. After plowing, soil looks bumpy and is dark brown.

metal blades

tractor

plow

hitch

turned over soil

Down in the dirt

A tractor pulls a plow. It takes a lot of power to dig and turn the soil. A tractor must have a powerful engine to get the job done.

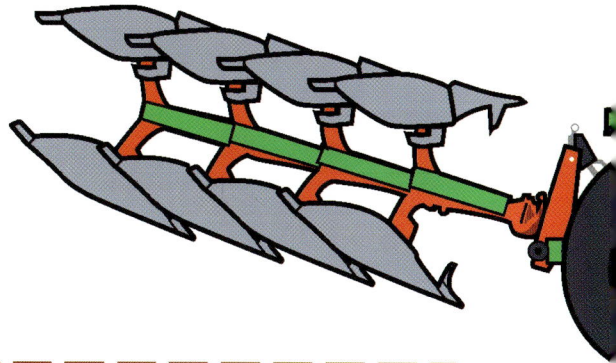

Big tires help tractors pull plows on soft or muddy surfaces.

Cultivator

A **cultivator** breaks up the big chunks of soil left behind by the plow. It is sometimes called a harrow or a soil finisher. A tractor pulls the cultivator.

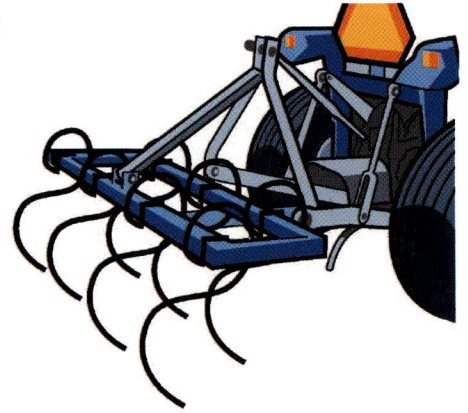

What a drag!

Some cultivators have a frame with metal tines, or curved bars, that are dragged along the ground to break up the soil. Some also drag a metal wheel called a crumble roller that breaks the soil up even more.

cultivator

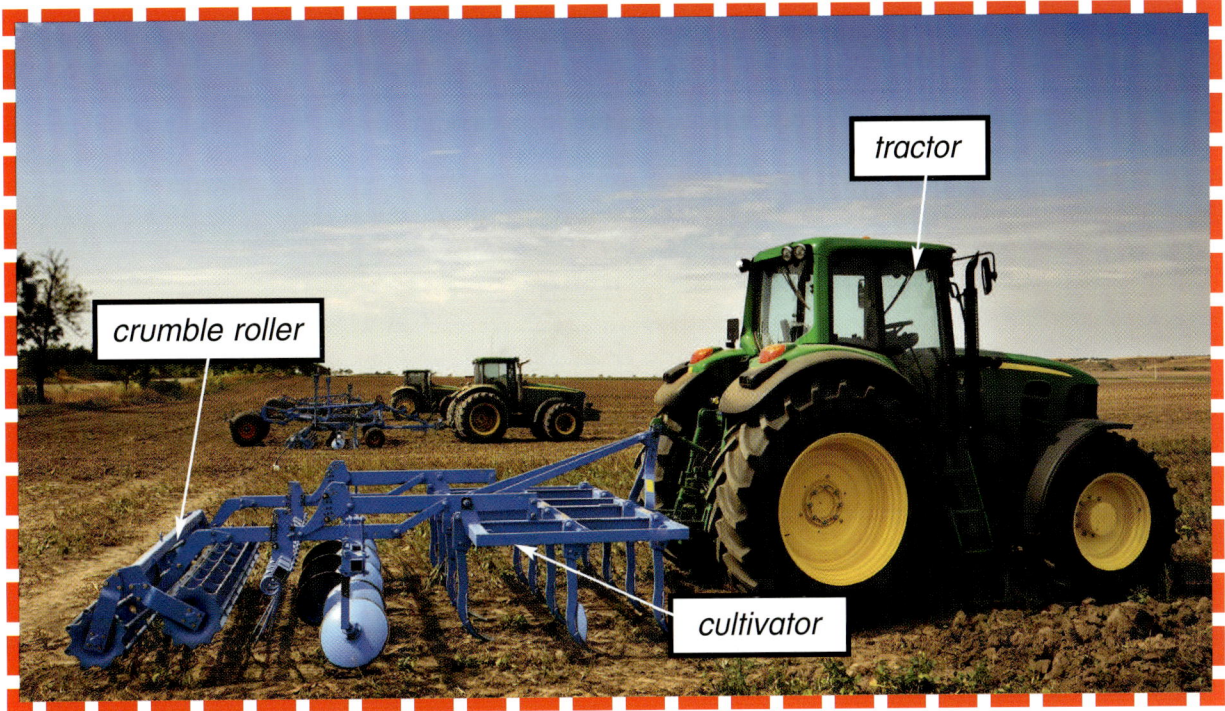

tractor

crumble roller

cultivator

These tractors will cultivate a big field together.

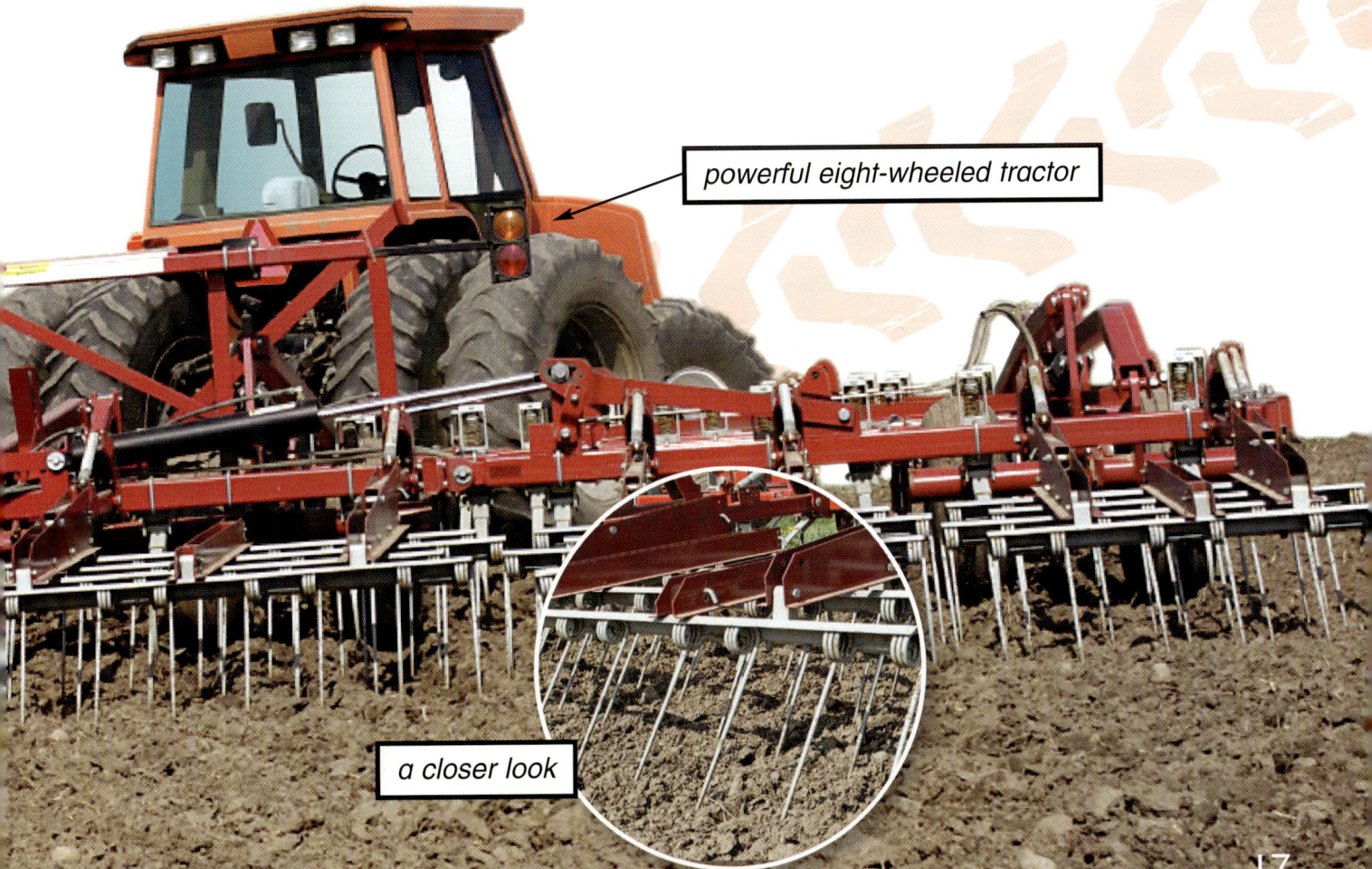

powerful eight-wheeled tractor

a closer look

Manure spreaders

A **manure spreader** does just what its name says. It spreads manure over soil. Manure is the waste from animals. Manure is good for the soil. It adds food and nutrients for growing crops.

shredders

manure spreader

Smelly stuff

A manure spreader hooks up to a tractor by the hitch in the back. The PTO gives it the power it needs. Keep a good distance away! Some machines have a spinning wheel with paddles on chains that throw out the manure over farmers' fields.

A pile of manure ready to be loaded into manure spreaders.

A manure spreader throwing manure over a field. The smell in the air is probably not so great!

Seed drill

The **seed drill** has a bucket, called a hopper, filled with seeds. A sharp drill cuts holes in the soil. A seed drops down from the hopper through a tube and into the soil. A wheel or tine at the very back of the seeder covers the hole and seed with soil.

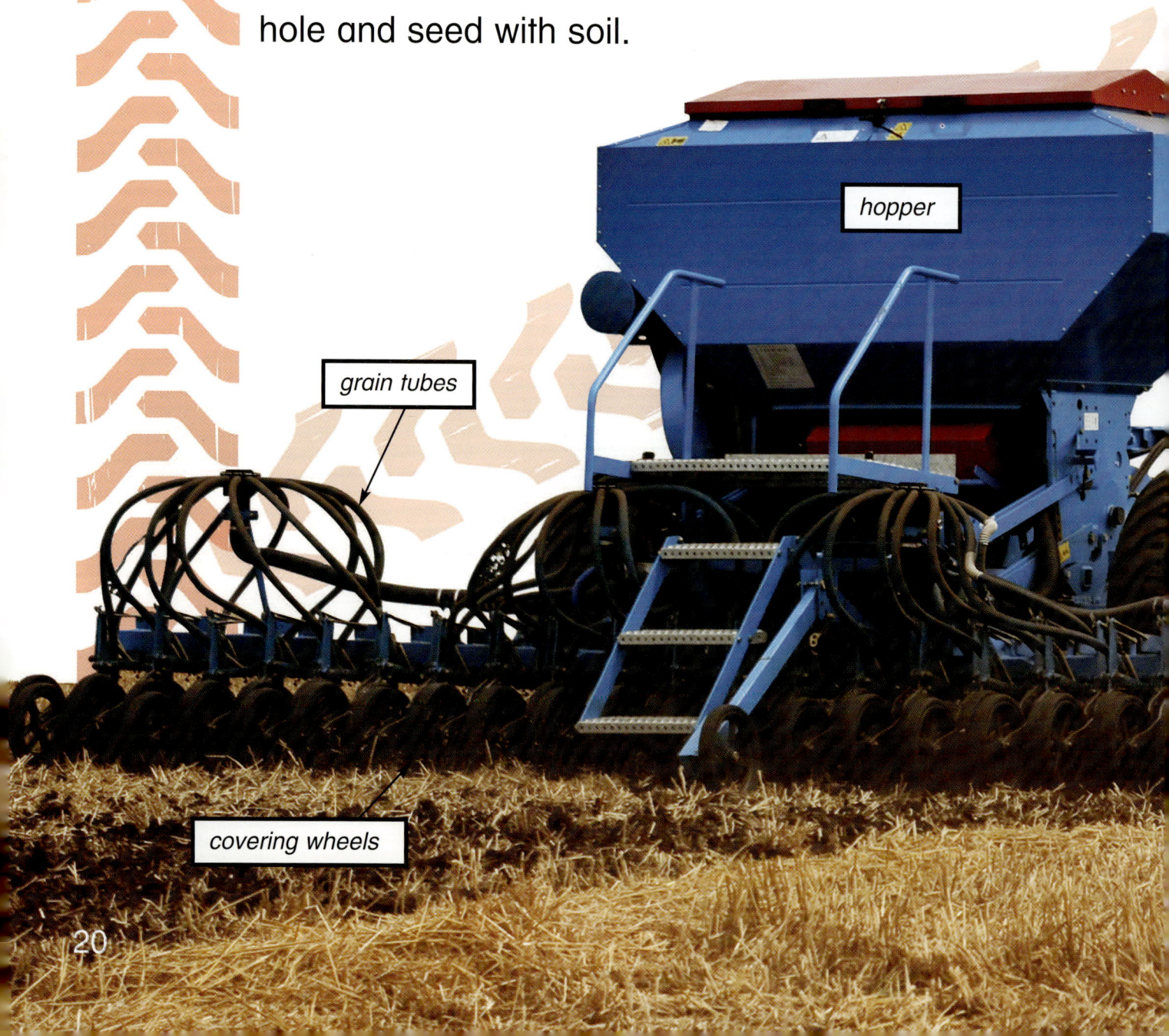

hopper

grain tubes

covering wheels

Lining it all up

The seed drill plants seeds in neat, straight rows. It is pulled through the fields by a tractor and gets power from the PTO.

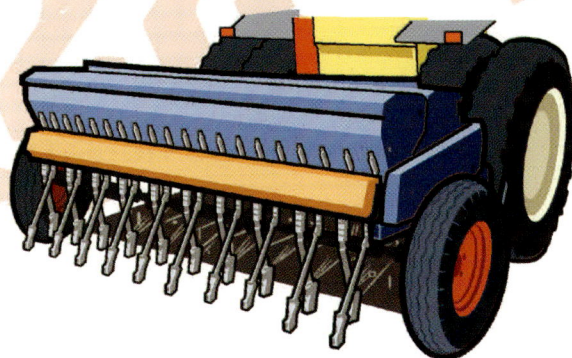

tractor

press wheel

Watering machines

Plants need a lot of water to grow. Rain waters a crop. When it does not rain, farmers water fields with irrigation machines. Irrigate means to water.

pivot irrigation machine

Some farms use pivot irrigation machines. They have their own electric motor to move them around a field.

Keeping it wet

Some **watering machines** are pulled by a tractor. They have a hose that hooks up to a water tap in the field. The tractor pulls a rain gun that shoots water into the field like a big lawn sprinkler.

Tractors and trucks with rain guns can water large vegetable and grain fields.

hose reel

hitch

tractor

Some farms use hose reel irrigators. Tractors pull them across farmlands to places that need watering.

Crop sprayers

Crop sprayers spray crops with pesticides and fertilizers. Pesticides are liquid chemicals that protect crops from insects, diseases, and weeds that could destroy them. Fertilizers are nutrients that are used to feed crops.

Some crop sprayers have big and tall wheels. They can drive over tall crops.

Insects, beware!

Some crop sprayers are pulled by tractors. A big tank holds the liquid pesticide or fertilizer. Some have pumps that draw the liquid from the tank. A hose sprays the fields evenly.

Crop sprayers are used to spray fruit trees, too.

tractor

tank

spray unit

Harvesters

Harvesters are large vehicles that pick, or harvest, crops. Farmers harvest crops when they are done growing. Different harvesters bring in different kinds of crops. Some can be attached to tractors. Others are vehicles that are driven over fields.

truck collecting potatoes

potato harvester

tractor

Potato harvesters dig potatoes out of the ground. Harvested potatoes are then uploaded to a truck or a trailer.

Above and below

Some harvesters gather crops that grow underground, such as potatoes, carrots, or beets. A grape harvester is a vehicle built to pick grapes in large vineyards.

grape harvester

grape vine with grapes

Combine harvester

A **combine harvester** is a big vehicle that gathers crops such as wheat and corn. A cutter bar in the front has sharp blades that go back and forth. This cuts the grain. The driver sits in a cab behind the cutter bar. The cab has large windows so the driver can see all around.

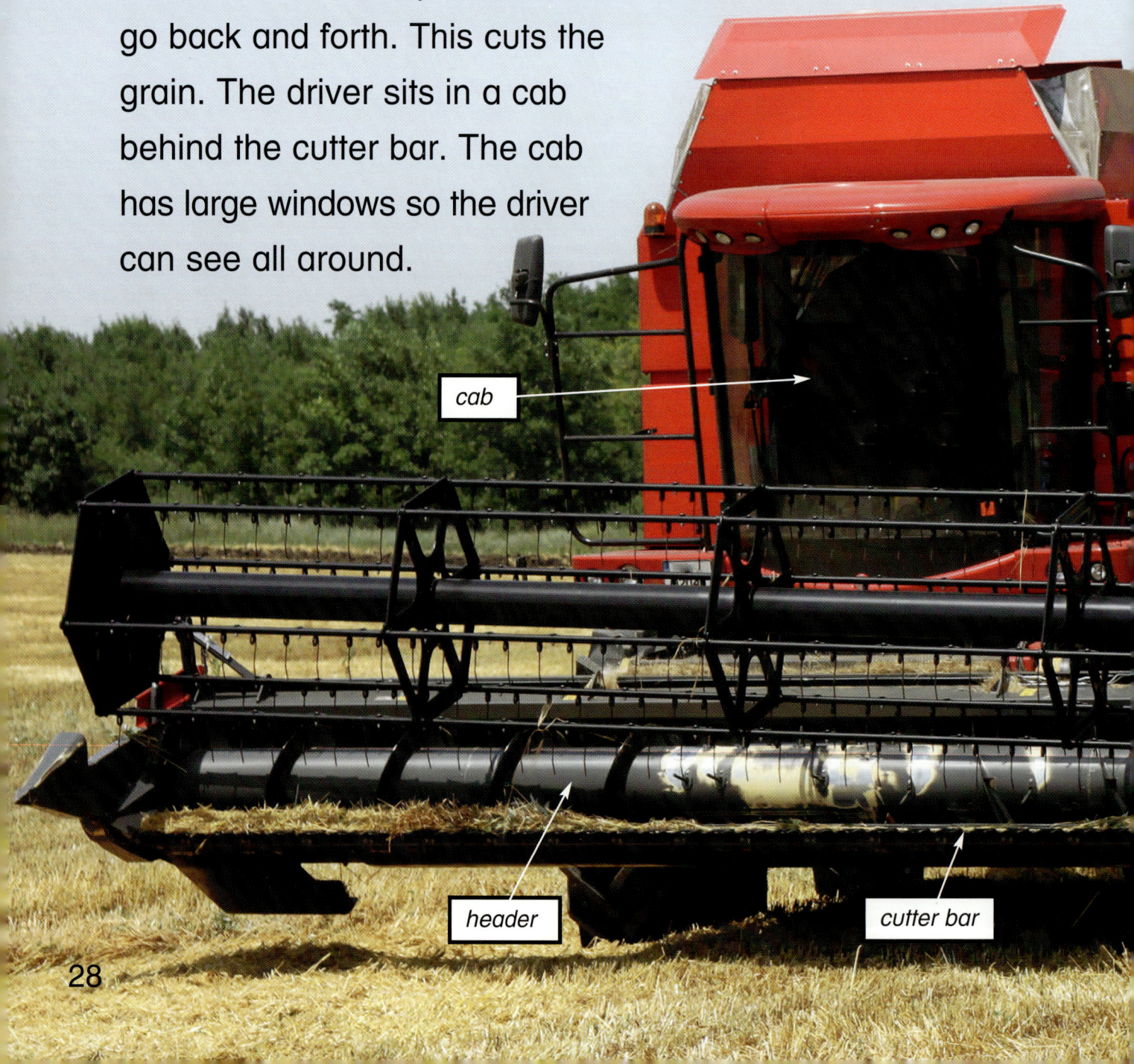

cab

header

cutter bar

What goes on inside?

After the crop is cut, it is sucked into the harvester. Inside, the grain is threshed, or removed, from the stalk. The grain moves into a holding tank. The rest of the stalks are thrown out of the harvester onto the ground behind. The harvested crop can be unloaded into a trailer while both vehicles continue moving and working.

unloading tube

holding tank

trailer

tractor

Hay baler

A **hay baler** collects hay or straw and packs it together in a tight bundle. Hay is grass that has been mowed, or cut, and dried. Straw is the leftover stalk from harvested grain crops. Hay is used to feed horses and cows. Straw is bedding for animals.

circular hay baler

Round bales of hay are big and heavy. Some bales can weigh as much as 2,205 pounds (1,000 kg).

Putting it all together

Tines or prongs lift loose hay into the baler. Inside, hay is packed together tightly. When the bale is done, a net or a string called twine is placed around it to keep it together. The baler pushes the bale out on the field. There are different kinds of hay balers. Some make large round bales of hay. Others make rectangular bales of hay.

rectangular hay baler

Rectangular bales of hay are easier to transport and stack on top of each other than round bales.

Words to know and Index

combine harvesters
pages 28–29

crop sprayers
pages 24–25

crawler tractor
page 11

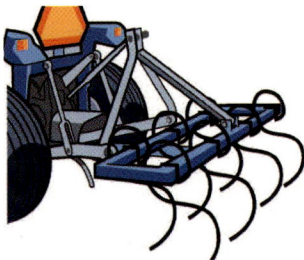

cultivator
pages 16–17

harvesters
pages 26–29

hay baler
pages 30–31

hitch
pages 7, 14, 19

plow
pages 14–15

manure spreader
pages 18–19

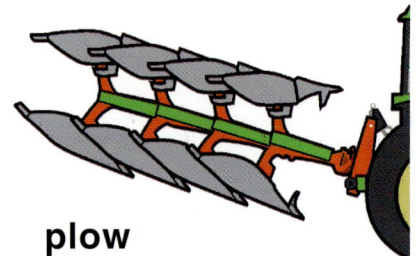

tractor
pages 6–13, 14, 15, 16,
17, 19, 21, 23, 25, 26

seed drill
page 20

Other index words
CUT 12–13
PTO 7, 19, 21
watering machines
22–23